Christmas
Bucket

By Timothy Allred

I would like to dedicate *Christmas Bucket* to my wonderful wife and my three amazing children. *Christmas Bucket* is full of real experiences we had as a family. We had a lot of fun reading it together. My kids were excited to see themselves in a story. I tried to capture their personalities and how we interact as a family. I wanted to write something like this for a while. I have read several Christmas books and started to think of ideas. Once I started, it came fast. I felt like I was writing and reading a book at the same time. I was inspired by God while writing *Christmas Bucket* and hope you enjoy it.

CONTENTS

1

College Graduation

Ashley and I were broke college students with a young family. We had three children – Emma, age 8, Kaylee, 6, and Eli, 4. We were a loving family, but like all families, we had our challenges. We lived off $5 Hot-N-Ready pizzas, rice, beans, and whatever was on sale. To save money, I even had water with my cereal instead of milk.

As graduation day came closer for both of us, we realized our simple, broke, college life was about to end. We discussed where we wanted to live, job opportunities, and what we wanted for our family. Ashley is an amazing mother. Early on in our marriage, she told me she wanted to be at home as much as possible, even if that meant putting off her career. Things seemed bright for us, but our bank account was empty, and we had little to live off.

After many prayers, we decided to move to Great Falls, MT. Two days before graduation, Ashley and I had not found an apartment there, but housing was more affordable, and jobs were available. We had $450 saved in our sock drawer. We spent the last two days calling every landlord that we could. There were openings, and some of them had 2-bedroom apartments for $400, but without a deposit and a job lined up they couldn't promise us anything. I became more and more stressed.

It was December 1st. I should have been excited, but I couldn't relax knowing that we needed to be out of our current apartment after graduation on December 3rd. Where was my family going to live? Where would I work? How would I provide food for us? So many unknowns.

Ashley was busy the last few days trying to pack everything. I still had two exams to take. One day, I studied long hours and was at the library late into the night. I came home and told Ashley how tired I was. How stressed I was. I was so caught up in myself I didn't even kiss the kids goodnight.

Ashley turned to me and said, "How dare you? I took my last exams two days ago and I have been working nonstop packing. You haven't asked how I was doing."

I didn't know what to say, I had only been thinking about poor me. I hadn't taken the time to consider her thoughts and what she needed. The house was full of boxes: boxes with onesies, princess and superhero pajamas, and house belongings. In one of the boxes was a picture of Ashley and I when we were newly married. Our eyes were full of innocence and new love. Full of hope and passion. And now, as I sat in my bed listening to my wife, I realized I had forgotten to think of her these last few days. I never congratulated her on passing her exams. I hadn't thanked her for dinner or the words of encouragement she often spoke. No, I had only been thinking of myself. I quietly turned to my wife and apologized for the way I had been acting. I took her soft hands in mine and promised her I would be better. She leaned up close to me and snuggled into my arm. Tomorrow would be a new start. I would take my final exams in the morning then find something nice to do for my bride while I continued to look for an apartment.

After my exams, I felt a great peace. Looking back on the last four years of college and everything that we went through while raising a family and trying to keep up with all the demands of school brought me a feeling of accomplishment. Not only was I leaving with a degree, but also with an amazing wife and three kids. At that moment, I knew that my family was my biggest accomplishment. I felt good.

As I walked home, I noticed the most intriguing pinecones I had ever seen lying on the ground, almost calling me by name. They had a cool shape, were solid, and reminded me that a simple gift of love is what is needed most. I picked up four of them and took them home. I never thought the kids would be so excited about pinecones, but they were. They gave me hugs and kisses. Turning to face my wife, that same glow in her eyes that was in our wedding photograph was back.

She congratulated me on passing my exams and took a pinecone. She looked at it for a while and finally said, "This will do for now, but in the future, I would prefer something with more glitter or just chocolate." We laughed so hard my stomach began to hurt.

I turned my attention to finding an apartment. After searching all day, we had no luck. Finally, we had no choice. We began to prepare to move by loading up our truck not knowing where we would end up in Great Falls.

2

The Move and the Miracle

We woke up early and finished cleaning the apartment, knowing we wouldn't get our deposit back. No one ever did. We ate a good breakfast and went to graduation. Ashley's and my names were called shortly after one another. When she walked across the stage, I watched the most beautiful person I had ever known accept her diploma. Tears began to flow down my cheeks. I watched her as she walked back to her seat. I couldn't quit looking at her. She was a queen, my queen, and then someone said, "Sir, it's your turn."

They had to say my name twice. We often joke that they said my name twice because they couldn't believe I had graduated. It was an amazing graduation. They talked about our future and what laid in store for us. I sat there so excited until we walked outside.

There was my truck, full of stuff, nowhere to go, my little family piling in. My kids were looking at me and my wife, saying with their eyes, "We trust you Mom and Dad. We trust that you will take care of us and provide for us." So, off we went with little money, an old phone that had a few minutes on it, a packed lunch, and no house or job in sight.

It took us six hours to drive to Great Falls. We arrived around 4 p.m. with no idea what to do. Ashley suggested we call a local church and see if they had any thoughts. I was about to call when the kids said they had to use the bathroom, so we went to a gas station. I showed the kids where the bathroom was. Even though they were independent, I still worried about them. I worried about Eli the most. He often got distracted looking at things or talking with someone. I went with Eli into the men's bathroom and Ashley went with the girls.

Walking into the bathroom, a paper caught my attention — a flier for someone renting their basement out. It had three bedrooms, one bathroom, and included utilities. However, the price wasn't listed. Eli pushed me out of the way and said, "Dad, I gotta go!"

I was sure the price was too high, so I decided I wasn't going to call. I finished helping Eli, and kept him focused, and we walked out of the store.

In the truck, Ashley turned to me and said, "I saw a flier outside the bathroom door for a three-bedroom basement apartment. I wrote down the number. I think we should call."

"I don't think we can afford it," I replied.

"You never know. Just call it, Timothy."

I picked up the phone and called the number.

"Hello," said the lady who answered the phone.

"Hi, this is Timothy, and we are looking to rent your basement apartment."

"I don't know what you are talking about," she said. She was very nice, but said she wasn't renting out an apartment.

I went back into the store to see if the number Ashley wrote down was correct. It was one number off. I called the number and found out the apartment was going to be $700 a month with a $700 deposit. I pleaded my case, they said they understood, but there was nothing they could do for me. I sat in the truck defeated. Ashley tried to call a local church, but no one answered. We had enough money for a night in a hotel, but then we couldn't possibly pay rent.

Emma said, "Can we pray, Dad?"

I said sure, but I wasn't in the mood for praying.

"Heavenly Father, please bless my Dad. We love him. He is the best Daddy in the world. Amen."

I said "Amen." Now what? The phone rang as I was starting the truck. It was the lady that we called about the apartment that was the wrong number.

"Excuse me," she said. "I am sorry to call you, but you said you were looking for an apartment. Is that correct?"

"Yes," I said.

"Well, it turns out that I do have a possibility of something to rent, if you are interested."

"Yes, yes!" I said, "It doesn't matter what it is." She gave me her address and told me we could come by.

As we drove up to the house it was already dark outside. An older lady came out.

"Hello, I am Lynn."

"Hi," I said, and introduced myself and my family.

She looked at us and said, "You must be tired, please come in."

As we entered the home, she brought out a container of cookies and handed them to the kids. I don't recall them ever looking so happy to eat a cookie. I also ate one and had no complaints.

Lynn told us they had an old building in the back that used to be a church but was converted into an apartment years ago. She said no one had lived in it for a couple of years, but she kept good care of it. She said that she decided not to rent it out anymore, but when we called, she heard something in my voice. Something that made her call us back.

I explained our situation. She thought for a moment and then smiled at us and said, "$450 a month would be fine. It has three bedrooms and a nice little kitchen. I can show it to you first, if you'd like."

I didn't care what it looked like. I said, "I don't need to see it first, we'll take it."

I went to pay her, she smiled and said, "The first month is free. Consider it a Christmas gift."

Ashley hugged Lynn so tight I thought Lynn was going to pass out. With the feelings only a mother can express, Ashley said, "Thank you."

It was getting cold outside, and the sun had set hours ago. Lynn took us to look at the apartment. It had a steeple; the steeple wasn't very big, but you could tell it used to be a church.

I said to myself, "This is so cool."

As we walked into the church, or our new apartment, Emma said, "I knew we would find a place after we said prayers."

I thanked Emma but had no idea the Guy Upstairs would put us in a church! I went to church, when I was able to, but man, I thought, He's got me in church now! We loved the apartment. It was a lot bigger than our last one, but still felt cozy.

After we unloaded our boxes from the truck into the apartment, we laid blankets and sleeping bags on the floor. Lynn insisted she could find us some furniture, but it was too late that night. We gathered our family together in our new house. We left our old one having no idea where we were going to sleep, and now we had a home. Before bed, our family said a prayer of gratitude and quickly fell asleep.

3

New Job

I woke up early the next morning and started planning my day. My next step was to find a job. I quickly got out of bed and drove to a local store. I bought a local paper and opened the job classifieds. Most businesses didn't use the paper to advertise, but I didn't have a computer and hadn't heard back about other jobs I already applied for.

The second job in the listing was for a package handler at a local delivery company. It wasn't what a recent business graduate was looking for, but it was a job. I called the company, sure no one would answer at 6 a.m., but I didn't know the hours of a delivery company.

"Hello," a man answered.

"I am calling about the package handler position."

"Do you have a clean record?"

"Yes," I said.

"Then come over right now, two people didn't show up this morning."

"Yes, sir."

I drove to the warehouse and was met by Zach, the manager I spoke with on the phone. He had me fill out some paperwork and an application. After twenty minutes he said, "Are you ready to work?"

"Now?" I asked.

"Yes, now. It's the holidays, and we need to unload these packages from the trailer as fast as we can. We need warm bodies, and far as I can see, you have a warm body. Hours are 5 a.m. to 10 a.m. Monday through Saturday, with the option to work evenings."

I took off my coat and walked inside the warehouse where they were unloading the boxes.

"Well, jump in the trailer, don't break anything, but move, and move fast! We're already behind. I can't thank you enough for showing up!" Zach said.

***

When I pulled up to our new house at 10:30 a.m., a big truck was outside. I walked inside and saw several women and men setting up beds and furniture.

Ashley ran over to me. "Where have you been?"

"Uh," I said.

"Never mind, Lynn called her church last night and these folks got together to help us out. Isn't it amazing?"

"Yes, yes, it is." I jumped in and helped set up the beds up and move furniture around.

Kaylee was playing with some of the toys we brought. She liked dolls, but more than anything she loved horses. She would play with them all day if she could. Emma would often play 'mom' with the dolls while Kaylee would be the farm animals. She could even make a pig sound that made us all laugh. Eli watched his sisters, waiting to destroy whatever they made. Ashley and I thanked everyone so many times. Then I looked back and saw Lynn standing behind us. I gave her a big hug.

She said, "You hug a little harder than your wife."

"Sorry," I said. "We are so grateful for everything you have done."

"Helping people is why we are here on this earth. My late husband, Ken, would have made you sleep in the house last night. I hope your family enjoys their time here."

"I am sure we will," I said.

Lynn left and went inside. I couldn't believe it. Yesterday looked so dark and today looked so light.

After lunch Ashley said to me, "You didn't have a chance to tell me where you were this morning."

I told her about the job and how he put me to work immediately. "I think it will be a good job until I can find something else. I get off at 10 a.m., so it gives me time to look during the day."

"Tree!" Eli yelled.

We turned to look and there was a Christmas tree in our front room. In all the excitement we failed to see the tree that was set up. It didn't have any lights or ornaments, but there was a shiny bucket under the tree. It looked a little out of place but considering we didn't have anything else to decorate with, I decided it looked perfect after all.

"A humble tree with a humble bucket," I thought.

4

Hope

The next day was Sunday, December 5th.
With an invitation from Lynn, we decided to join
her at church that day. The church was in full swing
for Christmas. They had a tree in the foyer all lit up
with a shiny bucket under it. The choir was
practicing Christmas hymns. The spirit of Christmas
was alive in church that day. Everyone was nice and
kept asking about our family and our apartment.

After church, we headed home. On the way
Ashley asked to stop by the local school. She was
going to sign Emma and Kaylee up for school and
wanted to see what it looked like. We walked
around the building. It was a good-sized school
with new playground equipment. It had a tall slide
and big swings. Eli was excited about the short
basketball hoop. I found a ball that was left on the
playground and passed it to him. It hit him right in
the face. Good thing it was soft. He picked it up and
threw it into the air. It didn't hit the rim, but he
didn't care. He walked over to me holding the ball. I
lifted him up in the air so he could easily make a
shot. The ball bounced on the rim, but went in.

"Nice job!" Kaylee yelled.

Emma was going down the slide for the
tenth time when we told her we had to go.

After we got home, I looked at the Christmas tree and shiny bucket under it and said, "God, you have blessed me and my family so much. Thank you." I looked up at the ceiling of the old church and wondered how many prayers had been said in here.

The kids were tucked in early that night. We were all tired. I worked the next day at 5 a.m. and I had to get up at 4:30 a.m. I kissed Ashley goodnight.

She turned to me and said, "This is going to be the best Christmas ever."

"It already has been," I said.

5

The Bucket

Work was tiring but rewarding. It seemed like the day flew by. Zach told me I was doing a good job and said I was more of an elf than a package handler.

I thanked him and said, "That must make you Santa Claus."

He didn't laugh and walked away.

As I walked out the door to head home that morning, he yelled from his office, "Ho, Ho, Ho!"

I spent the next few days looking for jobs with no luck. Emma and Kaylee were enjoying school. Kaylee really liked her teacher.

"She has long blond hair and is really pretty," Kaylee said.

One day they came home with some homemade ornaments for the tree. As they were putting them on the tree, Eli picked up the bucket and put it on his head.

My wife laughed and said, "Eli, you are too big to be an ornament!"

Everyone started to laugh.

Lynn was so kind to us. She brought us baked goods and invited us again to church. There is something about baked goods and being invited to church that go together and I am totally fine with that. Other than Ashley, Lynn made the best brownies I have ever had. They had caramel on the inside.

I was on my fourth one when Emma said, "You better stop, or you are going to get a tummy ache."

She was right.

The next morning was Sunday, and we went to church. The tree was still in the foyer and the choir was singing even louder this time. As we were going to sit down, Ashley noticed a young lady in the back row by herself.

"I will be right back," Ashley said.

After five minutes of me wrestling Eli to his chair, Ashley returned.

"What was that about?"

"Oh, she looked lonely, and I thought I would introduce myself. I got her number and told her I would call her. She is also new to Great Falls." Ashley had a way of always befriending those in need.

That night we sang my favorite Christmas song, "Silent Night." We sang so loud we thought the windows would break. Eli made us sing it again, just for good measure. After the kids went to bed, I looked at the tree and the bucket before turning off the lights.

6

Twelve Days until Christmas

The very next day would be a day never to forget.

It started off like any other day. After work, I decided to come home instead of job searching.

Ashley met me at the door. "You have to come see this," she said enthusiastically.

Eli was behind her saying, "Hurry, hurry!"

I came into the front room. Ashley picked up the bucket. "Look inside."

Inside was an envelope and some money. "Who gave us this?"

"No one. I dropped off Emma and Kaylee at school and came home. A couple minutes later Eli came in carrying this," she said. "He gave it to me and said, 'Look, Mommy.' I haven't opened the envelope. I was waiting for you."

"What do you mean no one put it there? Did Lynn put this envelope in the bucket?"

"I asked her, and she said no."

"Well let's open the envelope and read it," I said.

For 12 days you will receive $100 each day, and a name will be in the envelope. You must figure out who the person is and what they need that day. You can only use the money to help them. Any unused money will not carry over to the next day. Your family has been chosen to make an impact in 12 lives that need to be touched this Christmas.

The first name is Janet Smith.

"What? This is crazy!" I exclaimed. "Someone must have put this here. And who is Janet Smith?"

"I don't know who she is, but why don't we try and figure it out? Have you ever heard of the 12 days of Christmas?" Ashley asked.

"Yes," I said. "But what about the money and the envelope?"

"I don't know how the envelope got there," Ashley said, "but I still think we should figure out who Janet Smith is and what she needs."

"Okay," I said. "I will look in the phone book."

"Wait," Ashley paused. "I know who she is. She is Kaylee's school teacher!"

"What could she possibly need?" I asked.

"I have no idea," Ashley said.

We decided to go to the school. It was recess and the kids were outside playing. As we entered the classroom, we could see Ms. Smith in the corner, crying. Ashley walked up to her and asked her if she was okay.

Ms. Smith was startled. "Oh sorry, I shouldn't have been crying."

Ashley replied, "What's wrong?"

Ms. Smith felt a connection to Ashley, a lot of people do, and she started talking.

The year before there was a student in her class she loved greatly. She tried to help her. She would come to school with old clothes on and smelled like she hadn't showered. Ms. Smith bought her clothes and food. One day she gave her new shoes. The child was so happy, but the next day she came back to school with her old shoes on and a note from her dad. The note told her not to buy anything else for his daughter and her shoes were fine. Ms. Smith and Ashley both cried. Ashley listened to her for a long time and then came over to me and Eli. She introduced us to Ms. Smith.

Ms. Smith said, "Your wife is so nice. She listened to me in a time of need. You are a very blessed man."

After Ashley and I left the school, we had no idea what to spend the $100 on to help Ms. Smith.

"Money can't buy peace," Ashley said.

Then it hit me. "What if we could show her how many kids she has been able to help? We could make a scrapbook with pictures of the students and have them say something about Ms. Smith."

"That is an excellent idea," said Ashley.

We went to the principal's office and explained the situation and what we wanted to do to help Ms. Smith.

The principal thought it was a great idea but said, "We would have to get permission from the parents to take a picture of their child and put a quote in the book." The principal was nice enough to give us each parent's number. I nominated Ashley to call them all.

Ashley was able to get ahold of every parent except one. She was told that the child had been out sick, and the mom was usually at the hospital with her.

The other parents were excited and thought it was a great idea. They all knew how much Ms. Smith cared for their children. The principal said the children and their parents could meet at the school gym that night after Ms. Smith had gone home.

Ashley said, "Let's go to the craft store now and get supplies."

As we drove, she said, "This is so strange, Timothy. We woke up with a note and now we are having 22 students and their parents gather at the school tonight."

"I know, it is bizarre," I said. "Where should we get the pictures developed?"

"Does anyone print pictures that late? The letter said we must do it today."

Ashley was finding several items in the craft store that she thought would be good. She had a craft book and several cut outs to go inside. I decided to call around to see who could print the pictures for us. After the third call, I found someone. The photoshop in Walmart said they closed at 6 p.m., but after I explained the situation, the lady I spoke with offered to stay late that night. I thanked her and told her we would be there as soon as we could.

We picked up the girls on the way home from the craft store. Ashley was so excited to tell them the news.

"Wow, you are doing this all for my teacher?" Kaylee said.

"Yes, we are," Ashley said.

Ashley and I had decided not to tell them about the shiny bucket, the money, and the letter, but Eli kept saying, "Tell them about the bucket!"

"What bucket?" Kaylee asked.

After I told them the story, Emma spoke first. "I wonder what name will be there tomorrow?"

"Tomorrow," I repeated. I hadn't thought about tomorrow, even though the letter said this would happen for 12 days. Is this really going to happen tomorrow? I still couldn't explain how the money and envelope got in the bucket.

"We will see," Ashley said.

I looked at her cautiously. She just shrugged her shoulders.

"Let's just get through tonight," Ashley said. Ashley grabbed the camera and said, "Let's go."

We got there five minutes early, and within ten minutes, everyone was there. Each child had their picture taken and said something nice about Ms. Smith. The feeling in the gym was amazing. There was so much excitement.

Some of the parents asked, "Why are you doing this?"

I just said, "We felt it was the right thing to do."

Everyone agreed. As we left the gym that night, I felt a happiness from serving that I hadn't felt in a long time. I looked up at the stars and said, "Thank you for giving me tonight." I couldn't ask for more. My wife and kids were so happy.

Ashley and I decided to split up to save time. "I'll drop you off at the house, and I will get the pictures developed," I said.

"That sounds great. I will get as much of the book done as I can," Ashley said.

I got to Walmart just after 7 p.m. and ran back to the photoshop. As I came around the corner, no one was there.

"Oh, no," I said out loud.

Then I heard a voice behind me. "Are you waiting for me?"

I turned and looked; it was a Walmart employee named Erica.

"Yes, yes, I am!"

"I was just about to leave. I wasn't sure if you would make it," said Erica.

She helped me upload the pictures to their website.

After the pictures were developed, I said "Merry Christmas, Erica. You have really helped someone this Christmas."

Erica looked happy but sad at the same time. "No problem," she said, "It is good to help when I can."

When I got home Ashley had most of the book done. "All I need to do now is put the pictures inside," she said.

"Did we ever find out where Ms. Smith lives?" I asked.

"Yes, the principal gave me her address," Ashley said.

Within half an hour the whole family was in the truck and on our way to surprise Ms. Smith. When she answered her door, she looked confused but when she saw Kaylee, a big smile spread across her face. We said that the class made something special for her because she has helped so many kids.

"Here you go Ms. Smith," Kaylee said, holding out the book.

"For me? What is this?"

As she flipped through the book tears filled her eyes. "Earlier today, I was crying because I couldn't help a child, now I am crying because of all the children I have helped. How did you ever know this is exactly what I needed?"

"The bucket!" Eli yelled.

"What is that?" Ms. Smith asked.

"Never mind," Ashley said. "Let's just say, we thought you would like it."

"I love it!" Ms. Smith exclaimed.

After hugs and more crying we drove home with smiles on all our faces.

"I love how I feel right now," Emma said.

7

Eleven Days until Christmas

The next morning, I got up at 4 a.m. and rushed to the bucket. There it was! A $100 dollar bill and an envelope. I couldn't believe it, but there it was. I wasn't sure if I should wake everyone up or let them sleep before I had to leave for work in 40 minutes.

Suddenly, I felt a tug, "Daddy, are you going to open the envelope?" Kaylee asked.

"It's the bucket!" Eli yelled.

"Open it, Daddy," Emma said.

"Yes, Daddy, open it," Ashley said.

"Well, I guess everyone is up and is as excited as I am." I opened the envelope and read the name.

The second name is Greg Baxter

"Greg Baxter! Who is Greg Baxter?" I asked.

"I don't know," everyone replied.

After Ashley and I got the kids back to bed, I left for work a little early. As I pulled into the parking lot, I saw Zach sitting in his car. I walked by his car and his head was down. He looked up at me and smiled, but it seemed forced. I didn't think much of it at the time.

I went inside the warehouse and unloaded my packages, or Christmas presents, for hundreds of kids. As I did, I couldn't stop thinking about the new name "Greg Baxter." I asked my co-workers if they knew him, but they didn't know who he was either.

I asked Zach and he said, "Why do you want to know who Greg Baxter is?"

I couldn't tell him about the bucket, could I?

"I saw his name somewhere and my family was wondering about him."

"If my wife was wondering about another guy, I would be worried too."

We laughed, "It isn't like that."

"Whoever he is, if he needs a job, send him here. We still have one opening."

"Will do," I said.

While I was trying to figure out who Greg was, Ashley was too. After she dropped the kids off at school and got a big hug from Ms. Smith, she stopped by Lynn's house.

"Come in," Lynn said. "Have you figured out where the money and letter came from?"

"What, how did you know about that?" Ashley asked.

"You asked me about it yesterday."

"Oh, that is right. I forgot I asked you!"

Ashley told Lynn about our experience the day before and explained there was another name in the bucket this morning.

"You probably think we are crazy!" Ashley laughed.

"Just a little," Lynn said with a wink in her eye. "All I know is that God is using you for good in this world, and this thing you've got going on seems like His work."

"Thank you," Ashley replied. "You should have seen Ms. Smith's face yesterday and today. She was so happy. Her countenance was beaming."

"You are lucky to have this experience," Lynn said. "So, what name do you have for today?"

"Greg Baxter."

"I know Greg Baxter; he lives a couple doors down. He always decorates for Christmas. Lights all over his house. What are you supposed to do for him?" Lynn asked .

"I have no idea. Do you know anything about him?" Ashley asked.

"Well, I know he is very active in his church and has been super busy lately," Lynn said. Ashley thanked Lynn for the information and hurried home to tell me the news.

I walked in the house and Ashley said, "I know who he is!"

"You do?" I gasped.

"Lynn knows him. He lives down the street. Let's go to his house."

"And say what? He is going to think we are crazy."

"We don't need to tell him about the bucket. Let's just introduce ourselves and see if we find anything out. If it was anything like yesterday, you must reach out to someone to know what they need."

After we had some peanut butter and jelly sandwiches for lunch, we headed down the street. As we approached his house Ashley said, "That is strange."

"What's strange?" I asked.

"Lynn said he always decorates his house, but nothing is outside."

When we knocked, a young woman answered the door.

"Is Greg here?" Ashley asked.

"My dad is not home, and he has church meetings until late tonight."

"Church meetings?" I asked.

"Yes," she replied.

Right then the mother came to the door, "Can I help you?"

"Hi, my name is Ashley, and this is my husband, Timothy. We just moved into Lynn's church apartment. We are looking for some service opportunities for our family. Lynn said you normally have lights up. We are wondering if you need any help this year?"

"Well, that is nice of you. My name is Lacey. My husband has been so busy at church. He often meets with people to help them, and this Christmas has been especially busy for him. We couldn't ask you to set up the lights though."

"Do you still have the lights?" I asked.

"Oh yes, but they are in boxes in the shed," Lacey said.

"If I can find some help to set them up tonight, can we do it? We would like to surprise your husband."

"That would be amazing. He gets home at five, eats dinner, and then leaves again at six to go to the church. You can come over then."

As we walked back to the house, I said to Ashley, "You are amazing, I didn't know what to say when Lacey came to the door."

"You just keep saying that I am amazing, and you will be happy," Ashley said. We laughed, but then she said, "I am being serious."

"I have an idea. I'll go around the neighborhood at five and see if anyone wants to help," I said.

"Now that is an amazing idea," Ashley said as she kissed me. "I don't remember a time being so happy."

At five the kids and I left the house. Ashley stayed home to make cookies. As we walked through the neighborhood introducing ourselves, we found that several neighbors loved the Baxter family and were happy to help. A few of them said they had extra decorations and lights they would bring. By 6:30 p.m. about twenty people with headlamps and flashlights gathered outside the Baxter's home.

I knocked on the door, and Lacey answered, "He is gone. The lights are in the shed. I'll show you which boxes they are in."

We went to the shed and began working. Ashley met up with us and handed out cookies to everyone. Eli handed some out too, but he handed the most out to himself, and Ashley had to stop him from eating his sixth cookie. Lacey and her daughter came back outside with cups of hot chocolate. As we worked and the kids played, a few of us sang Christmas songs. By 8:30 p.m. everything was done.

"The house has never looked better, and where did all of these decorations come from?" Lacey exclaimed.

"From your loving neighbors," one woman said behind me.

Lacey's phone rang. It was Greg. "I am on my way home," he said.

We turned off all the lights and hid behind a tree. When Greg got out of his truck, Lacey turned on the lights, and we all yelled "Merry Christmas!"

"What is this?" Greg said, stopping and staring at his yard.

As Lacey explained his face lit up with joy. When he got out of the truck, you could see a weight on his shoulders, and now he seemed as light as a feather. We introduced ourselves and Ashley gave him a cookie. Greg thanked everyone and gave hugs to many. I looked back before we went home and saw Lacey, Greg, and their daughter holding hands as they stood outside looking at the lights.

After he got in his jammies Eli said, "I am sleeping next to the bucket!"

After several minutes Ashley was able to convince him that the bucket needed to be under the tree, and he needed to be in his bed for it to work right.

8

Ten Days until Christmas

At 4 a.m. I was wide awake. I went to the bucket and the kids were already there. They were too excited to sleep. Ashley was right behind me.

"Well, did it happen again?" I asked.

"Yes, daddy," they all shouted.

"Well, what should we do?" I asked.

"Open it!" they yelled.

I opened the envelope and read the name.

The third name is Zach Jones

"I know him," I said quietly.

"You do?" Ashley exclaimed.

"Yes, he is my boss." I sat there thinking for a few minutes. Everyone watched me.

"What are you going to do, Dad?" Emma asked.

"I don't know. Whatever needs to be done needs to be done today."

Slowly I got dressed and got ready for work. I pulled up and Zach's car was there, but he wasn't in his car. I found him talking to one of the truck drivers. I walked up to Zach.

"Good morning, Zach, how is everything going?"

"Hi, Timothy, this is one of our drivers, Buddy Brown."

"Hi, Buddy," I said.

"Good to meet you, Timothy. I'm dropping off a load and heading to another city. I am never in the same city for long."

"Timothy, you better get going, two of the package handlers called in sick last night. Looks like I will be joining you," Zach said.

"Sounds good."

I jumped in the trailer and started loading packages on the conveyor belt while the drivers started sorting through the addresses and loading the appropriate packages onto their trucks. A few minutes later, Zach jumped in.

"Thanks, Zach! How are you doing?" I asked the second time.

"Things are hard right now, but I don't want to worry you."

I didn't say anything at first.

About five minutes later he said, "My wife left me, and we recently got divorced. I had no idea that she wasn't happy. We just had our five-year anniversary, and she tells me there is someone else."

"I am so sorry," I said.

"I haven't eaten in weeks other than a few bites here and there. I had no idea how hard this would be. I miss her so much."

The rest of the morning we worked together, not saying much, but I wanted to. When we were done, I asked Zach if he wanted to go out for a late breakfast.

"I would," he said.

Zach got in my truck and started to cry. Not just tears, but with uncontrollable shaking and wailing. He was inconsolable.

"What can I do?" I asked Zach.

"I don't know. My life is so hard right now. The pain that I feel hurts my chest so bad. I wish I had someone to talk to."

"Zach, I am here. I know we just met, but this morning your name came up and I know that we needed to talk today."

As we continued to talk and I mainly listened, I realized how many people struggle with something every day. It seems like this earth is a big hospital and God is counting on us to be angel health care providers. We ordered our food, and the total came to $26. I told the waitress to keep the change.

"$74?" she exclaimed.

"Yes, I won't have it tomorrow anyway."

I drove Zach back to work and left him at his car. Zach and I exchanged numbers before I went home. I told Ashley about my day and told her that the assignment for day ten was done.

"I don't think so, Timothy. There is more to today's story. I feel like there is something else we need to do."

"I don't know what else I can do," I replied.

That night I decided to take a drive to the store. Zach's car was in the parking lot. I saw him walking with his head down.

"Zach!" I yelled, "What are you doing?"

Zach didn't look good at all. "I don't know, I am lost, this can't go on."

"What do you mean "this can't go on"? Are you thinking about ending your life?"

"It has crossed my mind several times tonight."

"Zach, do you mind if I stay with you tonight?"

"I guess. But why would you do that?"

"Because that is what friends are for."

"I need a friend," Zach said.

"Zach, do you mind if I call and find someone that you can talk to tomorrow, a professional?"

"Sure, but that stuff doesn't help."

I called around and found someone willing to meet Zach the next day. Zach agreed to the appointment. That night we sat by each other watching an old Christmas show about a boy and BB gun. We laughed and gave each other hugs.

"Ashley, I am not going to be home tonight, I will call you in the morning."

"I knew that God wanted and needed you to be there for him tonight. Spend whatever time you need. And Timothy," she paused.

"Yes?"

"I love you."

In the morning Zach and I left his house and drove to work. At 10 a.m., I was getting ready to leave.

"Zach, can I drive you to your meeting this morning?"

"That would be great."

After Zach's appointment, he turned to me and said, "I have hope. Thank you for giving me that hope."

"Do you mind if I call you to check on you?" I asked.

"Yes, you can call me. Every night if you want."

On my way home, I felt overwhelmed. The last few days had been great, but they had also been mentally draining.

9

Nine Days until Christmas

I walked inside and Ashley was sitting with Eli. Eli was holding the bucket. With a big smile on his face he said, "The bucket thing happened again."

"Honey, are you okay?" Ashley asked.

"Yes, but I am tired."

"Maybe I can do it today," said Ashley.

"Maybe," I said.

"The girls were sad they wouldn't be here when we read the name, but they understood."

"Alright, can you please read the name?" I asked.

Ashley opened the envelope and read:

The fourth name is nameless

"What?" I spoke. "Who is named nameless?"

"I don't know, but someone who is nameless needs us today," Ashley said. "Did you notice how nameless wasn't capitalized. Maybe it is representative of something else." She paused,

"Can you please watch Eli? I feel I need to go for a run to figure this out."

"Sure, but don't be gone too long, we'll need to work on this 'nameless' puzzle together when you get back."

It was a cold, windy afternoon for a run, but Ashley said she felt like this would help her find nameless. As she ran the streets, she headed downtown. She looked around and saw the stores decorated for Christmas. She saw people coming and going with packages in their hands. The snow was falling softly, but not enough to stay on the ground. She ran to the city building and saw a few people gathered in the park. They were sitting under a few trees for shelter from the cold.

Ashley wasn't watching ahead of her, and she ran right into a lady coming up the street. "I am so sorry!" Ashley said. "I was looking at those people in the park and didn't see you."

"Those people, they shouldn't be here. They don't have a home or a place to go and they take over the park. No one knows their names," the lady grumbled.

"What do you mean no one knows their names?" Ashley asked.

"Just what I said, no one cares about them, they are nameless," the lady said.

"Nameless," Ashley repeated.

"Yes, I must go, so please, love, out of my way," the lady said, stepping around Ashley.

Ashley looked at the ten or so people in the park that were not seen and nameless. She walked up to them. "Hi, I am Ashley. What are your names?"

It was quiet for a few seconds until someone said, "Jim." Then "Janet, Rob, Michele, Heather, Tanya, Chris, Matt, Ben, and lastly Wayne."

"You are not nameless," Ashley said.

"Of course, we have names!" Jim replied.

"Of course, you do. I am so sorry," Ashley said.

"We may not be seen, but we see you. We all have stories and backgrounds if you take time to get to know us."

"May I have a seat?" Ashley asked.

Heather replied, "It's a free world, you can sit where you want."

"Don't mind her," Jim said, "she can be a little coarse at times."

"I am sure life is hard for all of you," Ashley said.

"Yes, it is, but we are humans just like you. We have feelings and emotions. All of us had homes at one point, families, and even jobs." Jim laughed when he said "jobs." "I used to work construction."

"Why are you here?" Ashley asked.

"Now that is a long story. I have made a lot of bad decisions in my life. I have also made some good ones. When I was young my dad used to smack around my brother and me. I promised myself that I would be gone as soon as I could. When I turned 18, I was out. Out of the house and dropped out of school two months before graduation. I stayed at friends' houses until their parents said I needed to go. I found myself sleeping on the streets and stealing to eat. I got used to watching out for myself. I saw a lot of things during those days. Drugs, fights, rape, and even murder. It is a dark world, but we are all people with a story."

"Jim, if I could do one thing for you today, what would that be?"

"I would love to have a Christmas dinner. Potatoes, ham, rolls, salads, and pies. I love me some good pie."

"Okay, it's one now. I will be back tonight with Christmas dinner. Please let everyone here know that I will be back at six"

"Sounds good. I am looking forward to it."

Ashley walked away not knowing how she was going to make this happen. She ran home faster than she ever thought she could and told me the whole story. She was out of breath, bent over, and had to take pauses to finish it. Then she began giving orders like a sergeant in the military.

"You, get the kids from school; I will find a way to make this Christmas dinner for ten people with $100. Oh no, that is not going to be enough!" For a second, she thought about Jesus and feeding the five thousand. "But we'll make it work somehow."

Ashley showered and was gone. I walked to the school with Eli. As I waited for the girls to get out, I saw a catering company pull up to the gym. I asked a man standing by the catering van what was going on. He said there was an award banquet that night and they were providing dinner in the gym.

I asked how much it would cost to host a Christmas dinner for ten people.

"$20 a plate and a tip on top of that," he replied.

We didn't have enough money. I almost walked away, but at the last second Eli said, "Tell the man."

"Tell me what?" he asked.

I told him all about Ashley's run and meeting ten individuals that were homeless and that she promised them a Christmas dinner tonight on a budget of $100.

"That's quite a promise," the man said.

"Yeah, she is running around town trying to find anything."

"I don't think she is going to have much luck fulfilling that promise, but I hope she does," the man said. "Well, I better get the food inside."

"Can I give you my number in case something comes up?" I asked.

"I am not sure what would come up, but sure."

Eli and I walked away without much hope. We met the girls and walked home.

At five, Ashley walked through the door sobbing. "I didn't find anything. I even considered making them spaghetti, but that wasn't Jim's request. I asked everyone for help. I am not sure what to do."

Our little family gathered, and Emma said, "I will feed them. I can give them my favorite cereal."

"I love you honey, but that isn't going to work. I will have to go down there and tell them all 'sorry'. They all have names and are looking forward to tonight."

"Mommy, if the bucket says it is going to happen, it is going to happen," Kaylee said.

Just then our phone rang. It was the man from the catering company. He said, "A co-worker just called me, and she had another event cancel at the last minute. The food was all paid for, and they said they didn't want it. I told her I knew someone that needed it. Do you want it?" he asked.

I just about screamed, but managed to keep it in. "Let me ask my wife."

I told Ashley, who yelled, "Yes, yes, yes, tell the man yes!"

I made sure the man was still on the phone and said, "We'll take it."

"I know," he replied. "I heard your wife screaming. Where do you want my coworker to deliver the food?"

Ashley jumped on the phone and told him where to go and that we would meet his co-worker there.

"What is your name?" Ashley asked.

"I would like to be nameless if you don't mind. Makes me feel good to help and not have anyone know it was me."

Ashley couldn't help but laugh and said, "Of course, that is how this whole thing started today anyway."

"Grab your coats and shoes and let's go!" Ashley said.

We hurried out the door. We arrived a few minutes before 6 p.m., just in time to meet the van. We helped unload everything and set up. There were potatoes, ham, rolls, salads, and pies – lots of pies. Jim came over with his friends, Janet, Rob, Michele, Heather, Tanya, Chris, Matt, Ben, and Wayne for a Christmas dinner.

We sat around and talked to everyone and called them by their names. The kids sang Jingle Bells and Silent Night. They forgot some of the words to Silent Night, but everyone helped them out. The food was great. We had enough for everyone including our family. I tried to tip the caterers, but they refused. Ashley told me she would be right back. She returned with ten-$10 bills. "Merry Christmas," she said as she handed them out to Jim, Janet, Rob, Michele, Heather, Tanya, Chris, Matt, Ben, and Wayne.

We went home that night even more amazed at the miracles that continued to happen. Before I went to bed, I called Zach to make sure he was doing okay.

10

Eight Days until Christmas

At 4 a.m. I was awake again. We all were. We met at the tree. Ashley said I should open the envelope because it was my turn. I told her I didn't think that was how it worked.

"I have no control over this," I said. "I feel like my life is being worn out like an old catcher's glove."

"Daddy, open the envelope. What does the name say?" the kids asked.

I opened the envelope and read:

The fifth name is Crystal Robbins

"This looks like me again," Ashley said.

"You know Crystal Robbins?" I asked.

"I met her at church last Sunday. She was sitting in the back."

"Right, that seems like so long ago. What did she tell you? What does she need?"

"She didn't say much, I did get her number. She looked sad and probably needs a friend. I'll call her this morning while you are at work. Remember, this is the kids' last day of school before Christmas break."

I drove to work that morning thinking of Crystal Robbins. What would she need? I arrived at work and the first thing I looked for was Zach's car. It was there, but he wasn't in it.

I walked inside and he said, "Hi, Timothy. I wanted to give this to you."

He gave me a note and walked away. The note said:

"I think you saved my life. Thank you!"

I had to thank God for allowing me to be in Zach's life. Work went well. Zach helped me in the trailer again and before I knew it, it was time to go home.

When I walked in the door Ashley said, "We are going on a road trip!"

"We are?"

"Yes. We need to get the kids from school early and pick up Crystal. I will tell you all about it in the truck."

Eli jumped in the driver's seat. "I am driving," he said. I let him play with the steering wheel until Ashley came outside. "Time to get in your seat," I told Eli.

While we drove to get Emma and Kaylee, Ashley said, "I called Crystal and spoke with her for a while. Her mom died a year ago and she hasn't been able to go to her grave since the funeral. Her mom is buried in Kalispell."

"Well, I am glad we have $100 for gas then," I said.

We picked up the kids from school and drove to Crystal's house. Ashley went inside to get her, and we all piled into the truck. "Good thing this is a six-seater, Timothy," remarked Ashley.

With the three kids in the back and three adults in the front, Ashley squeezed right next to me.

"Thank you so much for taking me," Crystal said.

"We are happy to, Crystal. I have thought about you since church, and your name came up today." Ashley said.

Before we left Great Falls, we stopped at McDonald's and bought lunch. "Six double cheeseburgers, two large fries, and six waters please." I ordered.

Crystal loved kids, and it was amazing to watch her transform during the ride. She had a great smile and laughed with Emma, Kaylee, and Eli. Emma loved to tell stories and had many for this trip. She told Crystal she would have 90 kids and would live in a shed someday.

"If I am going to have 90 kids, I better meet my prince charming soon," Crystal said.

Kaylee promised her she would. Eli was busy with his Transformers. We drove by several lakes on the way to Kalispell, and Crystal started telling us about her mom.

"My mom loved to camp. She used to wake up early and make breakfast on her Coleman stove. We went for walks on the trails. She loved to sit by the fire and relax. She constantly told us the same stories and jokes. The best part about it was, she would laugh at them every time she told them. My mom had a sweet tooth. Several nights we would have s'mores, and if those ran out, we drove into town and would usually get a huckleberry ice cream cone. I miss my mom. I am so glad that you are going to be with me today. I am not sure why Ashley called me this morning, but I was praying to find a way to go to Kalispell with someone."

"We're happy to go with you Crystal," Ashley said.

I watched Crystal sit by her mom's tombstone for an hour. She cried, laughed, and talked to her as if she was there.

"I love you, Mom, and I will see you again soon." After Crystal said goodbye to her mom, she walked towards our family and said, "Mom said we need to get huckleberry ice cream cones. It will be my treat."

The kids screamed so loud. I was happy too. I love huckleberries. On the way home, Crystal asked Ashley what her favorite thing about being a mom was.

"There are many favorites, and hard days too, but today is one of the reasons I love being a mom. Being with my family is the most important thing. Having them be a part of your life, Crystal, and the memories they will have of this trip is all worth it."

It was getting dark now and the headlights of passing cars were making me tired. The kids were asleep in the back. Ashley was snuggling next to me, and Christmas music softly played in the background when we arrived at Crystal's house.

"Thanks again. It is a night I will never forget," Crystal said, as she shut the door.

I carried a 60 pound 4-year-old to his bed, his face full of the future. "Good night, Daddy," he said, before he closed his eyes and snuggled into his bed.

Before I went to bed, I called Zach to make sure he was doing okay.

11

Seven Days until Christmas

My alarm went off at 4:30 a.m. and I was surprised to hear it. I quickly turned it off. The house was quiet, so I knew everyone was still asleep.

"Long night," I said to myself. I got ready and headed to work without even looking in the bucket. I couldn't wait for work to be over. I kept thinking about the bucket and wanted to be with my family.

Zach saw that I was distracted and said, "Why don't you go home early today? I will jump in the truck and finish up."

"That would be great."

When I got home, I said, "Honey, I am home." Not a sound. Everyone was still asleep. I sat down in my chair and decided to take a nap until everyone woke up. Just as I was dozing off, Emma came into the room.

"Good morning, Daddy. I love you."

"I love you too."

I leaned back and fell asleep with Emma on my lap.

"Honey, it is time," Ashley said as she nudged my shoulder. "It's 9 a.m. and we need to look in the bucket." I opened my eyes and saw my whole family gathered around me.

"Daddy, can I look in it today?" Kaylee asked.

"Sure."

Kaylee opened the envelope and read the name.

The sixth name is Avery Burns

"Mom, I know her!" Kaylee exclaimed.

"You do?" Ashley asked.

"Yes, she is in my class."

"I don't remember her. We met everyone in your class," Ashley replied.

"Well, I haven't met her, but she is in my class. She has been out sick. I am not sure what is wrong with her," Kaylee said.

"I can call Ms. Smith and ask about her," Ashley said.

"Ms. Smith, this is Ashley. Kaylee was talking about Avery Burns, and I was wondering if you could tell me about her."

"Avery Burns is a very sweet girl. Earlier this year she was diagnosed with leukemia. She is getting treatment right now. Sixty years ago, almost no child survived this cancer, but now, almost 90% of children do. I have seen her a few times. Her mom doesn't like to talk about it. She is scared and doesn't know what to think. Sometimes I feel like Avery's the one giving her courage."

"That is so sad. Kaylee would like to do something for Avery today. Do you have any ideas?"

"I am not sure, but I know she loves angels. Let me know what you are going to do. I would like to be involved."

Ashley told us about the phone call and asked if we had any ideas.

"I do," said Kaylee.

"I do too," said Emma.

"Okay, one at a time. Kaylee, you go first," said Ashley.

"Since Avery loves angels, let's make her as many angels as possible."

"How would we do that?" asked Ashley.

"We could make her hundreds of snow angels outside her hospital room, so she could look at them."

"That is an incredible idea, Kaylee, but we don't have snow."

"We will. We also need to get the rest of our class together to do it."

"Okay, to have the faith of a child. Emma, what do you want to do?" Ashley asked.

"I want to write her a song."

"She would love that," Ashley said.

Ashley called back Ms. Smith and told her what the plan was.

"Well, I don't know if there will be snow, but if Kaylee says it will snow, then let's do it. I can call the class. I don't know how many will show up. We have 24 including Avery and Kaylee," said Ms. Smith.

"Eli and I will go to the store and see what we can get for Avery," I said.

Eli headed back to the Christmas section. They had several angel decorations for inside and outside the house, but nothing felt right. We were just about to leave when I saw Halloween costumes in the clearance section. There it was, an angel costume with a halo just Eli's size.

"Eli, what do you think about this?"

"Looks good to me, Dad, but I would rather be batman."

"This will be perfect. You can wear this when we go see Avery," I said.

As we left the store, I noticed something falling on my head. It was snow. Not only had it started to snow, but it was snowing hard. I could barely see on the way home.

"What do you think about that, Ashley? Kaylee knew it was going to snow."

Ashley was making a cake in the shape of an angel. "I just got off the phone with Ms. Smith, and every kid in class is going to be able to make it. I can't believe it."

"I can't believe this whole week," I said. I asked if she had spoken with Avery's mom.

"Not yet, I want to speak with her in person. I think it will be better that way. I will go there right now. I am so nervous."

"Hello Ms. Burns, can I speak with you for a second?" Ashley introduced herself and told her that Kaylee was in Avery's class.

"Call me Robin. I am so scared to lose my baby girl. I don't know what I would do with myself if something happened to her. I hate watching her in pain. We have some good days, and then we have a bad one. I don't know why God would do this to my little angel."

"This must be so hard. I have no idea how you feel. This morning we had a little miracle concerning Avery." After Ashley told her about the snow angels, the whole class coming, snow, and even Eli's angel costume, Robin started to cry.

"This is truly a tender mercy from God. I have wanted so badly to give her something for Christmas that she would remember. I will consider this God's Christmas gift to her."

Ashley and Robin hugged for several minutes. With tears streaming down her face Robin said, "Thank you."

The angel cake was frosted, Eli was in his costume, Emma had her song ready, and we were on the way to the hospital. There was a big field outside Avery's window where everyone met. The kids, adults, and some of the hospital staff all spread out. Avery looked out her window, and Ashley gave the thumbs up. We all fell to the ground and made snow angels for Avery. Then we jumped up and made some more. From Avery's room you could see hundreds of snow angels outside her window. She told her mom that those were like the angels she sees every day.

"Mom, can I go downstairs to thank them?"

"Yes, but you have to stay inside the door."

Everyone walked by the door and waved to Avery as she waved back. Ashley cut her a piece of cake, opened the door after receiving permission, and gave it to her. Avery looked like an angel herself. Her smile was so big. We were just about to leave when Emma said, "What about my song?"

They let Emma in the doors so she could sing the song she wrote for Avery:

Hey, we can tell you're feeling under the weather
But we're here to wish you to get better
We're praying for you night and day
We know God will light your way

"That is so beautiful," Avery said. "I did have angels light my way tonight."

"My mom helped me a bit, but I wrote most of it," Emma said.

"Thank you! Please tell everyone, thank you," Avery said.

On the way home Emma said, "As big as God is, He knows each one of us and what we need. We are his angels, aren't we, Mom?"

"Yes, honey you are – we all are."

Before I went to bed, I called Zach to make sure he was doing okay.

12

Six Days until Christmas

Sunday morning, we were all up again at 4 a.m. looking at the bucket and a new envelope inside it.

I said, "I am a little nervous to open it. Each name comes with a lot of responsibility."

"I will grab the envelope," Eli said.

"How about you open it," I replied.

As Eli opened the envelope, I read the name.

The seventh name is Bob Perks

"No idea," I said. "Anyone know Bob Perks?"

Everyone shook their heads no.

"Since it is 4 a.m. and I don't work today, let's go back to bed until church. Bob Perks. I wonder if he knows we got his name today?" I said to Ashley.

"I don't know, but he better get ready." We laughed and fell quickly asleep.

As we walked into the church, I saw a shiny bucket under their tree. I pointed the bucket out to

Ashley and said, "I wonder how many buckets are under trees right now?"

We asked a few people at church if they knew Bob Perks.

"No, never heard of him," was the response.

Church was great. They announced that they would be doing a live Nativity at the church on Christmas Eve and asked for volunteers. I asked Ashley if we should volunteer.

"No," she said, "we don't know what our assignment from the bucket will be."

"Bob Perks," I kept saying. Nothing was coming. Ashley looked on social media, nothing. We looked in the phone book, nothing. We asked Lynn, nothing. We were stumped.

I love to BBQ. For dinner we had hamburgers, hotdogs (Kaylee's favorite), pasta salad, watermelon (Emma's favorite), beans (unfortunately Eli's favorite), and chips. As I took the last bite of my hamburger, I told everyone I was going to go for a drive.

"It is getting late, and we still don't know who Bob Perks is," I said.

I drove around town. The sun was just setting. I wasn't thinking about much. I decided to turn into a gas station and then everything went crazy. Someone was honking at me. I looked over and a guy drove past me flipping me off. Unfortunately, I got upset and pulled behind him. He pulled off the road and so did I. I went to open my door and he started driving again. He turned around and came back by my truck with his window down. He was with a lady, and she looked embarrassed. He started to yell at me saying that he almost hit my truck when I turned suddenly.

For some reason I was very calm, and said, "I am sorry you almost hit me, but you shouldn't act like that. You had no reason to flip me off."

The lady in the truck put her hands up in a praying motion and whispered, "Thank you."

After a few more minutes everything calmed down. I introduced myself and he said, "I am Bob Perks."

He was about to drive off when I said, "Hold on. Bob, this may sound weird, but do you want to hang out tonight?"

I don't know who looked more shocked, Bob or his lady friend. "What are you thinking?"

"We could get a bite to eat." I didn't know what else to say even though I just ate.

"You know, Timothy, my daughter and I got into a fight tonight. She plays for the college basketball team, and I wasn't going to go. I know I should. Do you want to go to the game in an hour?"

"Yes."

"See you at the college then," he said.

I drove home to tell Ashley. As I unfolded the story, she said, "You could have been shot."

"I know. It was dumb but let me finish the story." I finished the story and asked Ashley if she would go to the game with me and Bob.

"Wait, first you almost fought this guy, and now you are going to a game together?"

"I guess that is how God works," I said.

"Someone has to watch the kids," Ashley said.

"What about Lynn?" I asked.

Lynn agreed to watch the kids. I wasn't sure if I should be scared to meet Bob at the game.

"Timothy!" Bob yelled, "Over here."

He gave me a hug with a pat on the back like we had been friends for a long time.

"Timothy, I am so sorry for the way I acted. That was not okay, do you forgive me?"

"Yes."

"Good, I needed to be here more than you know. I would have regretted it for the rest of my life if I didn't come. It is because of you that I decided to come."

I introduced him to Ashley, and he introduced me to his wife Kate. Kate quietly thanked me again. We walked into the gym, and they announced it was senior night. I didn't even need to ask; his daughter was a senior.

"Timothy, I forgot tonight was senior night. I will be right back." Five minutes later he came back with a bouquet of flowers. "Parents walk their kids to half court on senior night. My baby girl would have never forgiven me."

"Stacey Perks," the announcer said.

Bob and Kate were already down there. I saw them say something to their daughter and they each hugged. I watched a proud dad and mom walk with their daughter to half-court. After the game ended, they introduced us to Stacey.

"My dad said you were an angel tonight."

"I am not sure if I started out like a good one."

Bob and I looked at each other and then laughed.

"Must be an inside joke," Stacey said.

We wished everyone a Merry Christmas and started to walk away. Bob grabbed my shoulder and said, "Take advantage of every day with them. You never know when it will be the last or too late. Thank you again."

Before I went to bed, I called Zach to make sure he was doing okay.

13

Five Days until Christmas

At 4 a.m. we were at the tree again. No alarm needed. Everyone was there. Even the kids were wide awake.

"Dad, can I have a turn?" Emma asked.

"Absolutely."

Emma opened the envelope and read the name.

The eighth name is Erica Chambers

"Anyone know Erica Chambers?" Ashley asked.

"I met an Erica at Walmart recently, but that is the only one I know," I said.

Emma, Kaylee, and Eli didn't know anyone named Erica either.

Zach wasn't at work when I got there. At break time he showed up.

"How is it going, Zach?"

"Good, I was at my appointment this morning. It went well. I never thought I would like to speak with a therapist."

"We have to do what we need to do to survive in this life – no matter how hard it gets," I said. "Hey, I have to go to Walmart after work, do you want to go with me?"

"Sure," Zach said.

As we walked into Walmart, Zach said, "Why are we at Walmart looking for someone named Erica Chambers?"

"I can't tell you everything, but we will know by the end of the day," I said.

I found Erica back in the photoshop. I had learned to be bold this week.

"Erica, is your last name Chambers?"

"Yes, why do you ask?"

"Well, I was telling my friend that I met you last week and how kind you were to me. You stayed late and helped me upload and develop pictures. By the way, what you did was such a big hit. You helped someone more than you will ever know."

"That is nice of you to say."

"Yes, thank you, but that is not why I am here. My wife and I are going on a date tonight and wanted to go with another couple. Zach here doesn't have a date, and we are wondering if you would be his date tonight. So, will you?"

I didn't dare turn around. I could feel Zach's eyes on the back of my head.

"Well, I have a break in 5 minutes, I can speak with you and Zach then."

"Okay, great."

I turned to face Zach, and he looked red and pale at the same time.

"What were you thinking, Timothy?"

"She is cute, isn't she?"

"Yes, but, but…"

"But, what? You could go out with us and hang out with a cute girl. What is the harm in that?"

"You could have told me what you were doing."

"I could have, but I didn't know what I was doing until it happened."

"Seriously?"

"Yes, it just came to me."

"Hi, Timothy and Zach, it is good to meet you other than at work," Erica said when she met us for her break.

Zach was still foggy about what was going on, but he quickly snapped out of it. "Yes, it is good to meet you too."

"So, what would be the plans for the night, if I agreed?" she said, looking at Zach, who quickly looked at me.

"We thought we would go sledding and then get hot chocolate."

"That sounds fun," Erica said. "I haven't been on a date with someone for a while. I have never been asked out on a date by a stranger, for a stranger, but count me in."

By now Zach was trying to collect himself. He started to adjust his shirt and straighten his hair. "I may be a stranger, but I am no danger."

Erica laughed, but Zach tried to recover, "I mean. I am not sure what that was. That was probably the dumbest thing I have ever said."

I asked Zach where we should go sledding. He suggested Giant Springs Park.

"Giant Springs Park at 7 p.m. Does that work?"

"See you then," Erica said. "I am going to bring my dog; he doesn't like strangers." She laughed and we kind of laughed.

"I am not sure if I should thank you or fire you Timothy."

"Considering it is the holiday season, please thank me."

"Okay, thank you. That was crazy. You are a crazy guy."

"See you tonight at seven, Zach."

I dropped him off at work and went home. When I told Ashley the story, she almost fell on the ground she was laughing so hard. Emma and Kaylee started singing, "Matchmaker, matchmaker, make me a match."

I gave Eli a high five, and said, "That is how it is done." He started laughing as only a 4-year-old can.

Once again, we called on Lynn to babysit. She wasn't surprised. In fact, she said, "I was expecting this."

***

Before we went to the sledding hill, we had to buy sleds.

I said to Ashley, "If we buy these sleds with the money from the bucket, we have to give them away before we leave the hill."

We showed up five minutes late. Zach and Erica were already sledding together on one sled.

"Well, that happened fast," Ashley said.

"Hey guys," Zach said, "I got here early and so did Erica."

"Hi," said Erica, and she pulled a Shih Tzu out of her doggy backpack. "This is the killer I was telling you about. His name is Ryder."

"Cute dog. I am Ashley. This crazy guy's wife."

We spent a full hour sledding. We raced down the hill laughing and with snow flying in the air. After the sledding trip, we agreed to meet at Zach's house for hot chocolate. Zach gave Erica directions to his house, and they got in their cars and drove away. As we were leaving, we saw two kids sledding down the hill on their pants.

"Hey, do you two have sleds?"

"No, mister," one of them said.

"Here you go," Ashley said, and we walked away holding hands.

We went to Zach's. He said he had to speed to get home first to make sure it was clean.

"It is a good thing I have hot chocolate," he said.

We went out on his patio and looked at the stars while we sipped our cocoa.

"I better get going," Erica said. "I can't thank you enough for the invite. I have sat at home too many lonely nights." Zach volunteered to walk her to her car.

"So, did you give her a hug?" I asked.

"Yes, and we are going to get together next week."

"Nice! Zach is the man!" I declared.

He looked confused. "I still don't know how you knew her last name. This whole thing is kind of strange. Are you guys miracle workers?"

"You could say that," Ashley said.

"Whatever it is, keep doing it. It works for you."

Before we left, I asked Zach if he was doing okay.

After he closed the door, Ashley and I fist bumped, and clasped hands as we walked to our car.

14

Four Days until Christmas

"Daddy, get up," the kids said. "It's time."

I looked at the clock: 4 a.m. I slept through the night without waking up. Ashley was asleep too.

"We've done this for eight days, what is one more?" I thought. Ashley woke up and we got up with the kids.

"Open the envelope!" Emma and Kaylee yelled.

Eli just yelled, "Bucket, bucket, bucket."

I opened the envelope and read the name.

The ninth name is Buddy Brown

"Good old Buddy Brown!" I chuckled.

Ashley looked at me. "You know him?"

"Of course, we go way back to last week. We met once for two minutes. He drives truck and delivers trailers to the warehouse. Zach introduced us. I am guessing this one is mine too."

Ashley smiled. "You have had a few, but they always end up including me."

"Touché."

"Dad just said tushy!" The kids started laughing hard and kept saying, "Tushy, Dad said tushy."

"Good morning, Zach," I said I as I walked in. "Where is Buddy Brown?"

"Now how did you know Buddy was here? Wait, I probably shouldn't ask you too many questions. Do you have a date lined up for him too?"

"No, I just need to talk to him."

"He is in my office. He just found out his route has been delayed one day."

I walked in the office, "Hello Buddy, good to see you again."

"Sorry, I can't recall your name."

"It's Timothy."

"Right, how have things been going for you, Timothy?"

"I wish I could explain, but it has been an amazing ride this past week. Zach told me that your route has been delayed."

"Yes, it is the life of a trucker. I wish I could stay in a room and not have to sleep in the sleeper."

I told him my grandpa used to be a trucker and he had some wild stories.

"I have some of those too," Buddy said.

"Tell you what, Buddy, why don't I finish my shift, and then you can spend the day with me. We can spend the day in town and maybe even find somewhere you can stay tonight."

"Now why would you want to do that for me?"

"Because I want to. Isn't that a good enough reason?"

"I guess. That is awful nice of you."

"Just don't leave. I get done at 10 a.m."

"If you can't find me, check the truck," he said and let out a big laugh.

***

After work, Buddy and I drove to my house. "Buddy, I want you to meet my family. This is Ashley, Emma, Kaylee, and Eli."

"Is this the guy from the bucket?" Eli asked.

Ashley hushed Eli quickly.

"Buddy drives a truck across the country. He's the reason I have a job. He's the reason why so many kids will have Christmas this year."

"Well, I am not the only reason," Buddy said.

"Ashley, Buddy, and I are going to get some late breakfast or early lunch. Whatever you want to call it."

"Sounds good."

"I heard about a family diner that serves excellent food. Do you like steak and eggs?"

"Who doesn't?"

We arrived at the diner, sat down, and ordered our food.

The waiter said, "Your order should be out in about ten minutes."

"Buddy, you said you have some wild stories that you could tell me. Do you mind sharing?"

"Sure, where to start? I have been driving truck for several years. When I was younger, they didn't have Hours of Service like they do now. You could get away with things easier. The customer expected the load delivered by a certain time and they didn't take excuses. If you didn't make it, you would lose your job. There was always someone else willing to take your place. Sometimes they would try and monitor my hours because I was the fastest driver. I have driven all around the United States. I have seen this country grow up.

"One time, I brought my son with me. He was eleven years old, but he was a big kid. He was asleep in the sleeper, and I was getting a hard time on how fast I got to my deliveries. I told them I had an extra driver. They didn't believe me, so they went outside to check and saw my son curled up in the sleeper. I told them not to wake him because he would get angry if they did. I watched them slowly open the sleeper and shut it quietly. They came back and said, 'He is a big guy!'"

Buddy and I had a good laugh. The food arrived and we started to eat.

Buddy looked up from his food. "Timothy, I have to tell you another story that has changed my life forever. I have driven all kinds of truck, and this time I was driving a logging truck. I was going up this road and wasn't told that it wasn't safe. I found out later the road was giving out and a notice should have been posted. While I was driving up the road, the road began to give out. It was a long way down. I tried everything I could to stay on the road, but it was to no avail. The truck went over and so did I in the cab. I said to myself, "Well, this is it, Lord, if you want me out, it's up to you." Before I knew it, I was on the road watching the truck and logs tumble down the hill. God took me out of that truck. There is no way I got out on my own. I have tried to not be a disappointment and make my life worth saving. He saved me that day."

"I am sure that changed your life. Did you drive truck right after?"

"No, well, not that kind of truck. I drove a milk truck for a while. I loved talking to the people in town and seeing them. You get to know the folks in town and what makes them. Driving truck can be lonely. I miss that milk truck."

"Then why did you start driving truck again?"

"The world seems to move on even if you aren't ready for it. Everyone started buying milk at the store and a milk truck wasn't needed any more. I went back to what I knew, driving truck. I have had a good life, but I sure miss my late wife. We had a great life. One of our favorite things to do was square dance. Maybe in heaven there will be square dancing."

"Hi, Timothy." Lynn waved and walked up to our table.

"Hello, Lynn, this is Buddy Brown."

"Hello ma'am, I am everyone's buddy."

"Please, join us, Lynn," I said.

"Sure." Lynn sat in the booth with us.

"Buddy was just telling me he and his late wife used to square dance."

"I love square dancing too. Ken and I used to go all the time before he passed away."

"Is there anywhere in town that square dances?" I asked Lynn.

"Yes, there is one place in town that does, and I believe they are open tonight."

"You two should go," I said.

"I'm game, if you are, Buddy."

"You betcha! But let me buy you dinner tonight."

"Sure, but it isn't a date, I don't want Ken to be jealous that I am out with a cute man."

We laughed. Then Buddy looked at me, "What are you laughing at?"

We laughed some more.

"Buddy they also have a bed and breakfast if you need a place to stay. I've heard they make great breakfast," Lynn said.

Buddy turned to me and said, "This is going to be a night to remember."

"Just know, I have to be home by 10 p.m., Buddy. My parents said the Spirit goes to bed at night."

"Sounds like you have wise parents," Buddy said.

"They were the best. Those were different times. I miss them."

"Me too. Let's bring back as many memories as we can tonight," Buddy said.

"Deal," Lynn said.

I drove home by myself. Buddy and Lynn stayed at the diner and talked for hours before their dinner and dancing. I couldn't help but think the world just turned back fifty years to a simpler time. I told Ashley and the kids all about my experience with Buddy Brown. I felt like I had known him my whole life.

"There aren't too many men like that left." I started to cry a little, and Ashley put her hand on my shoulder.

"He definitely lived up to his name," she said. "He sounds like he is everyone's buddy."

Before I went to bed, I called Zach to make sure he was doing okay.

15

Three Days until Christmas

We all met at our usual location at 4 a.m.

"Good morning," I said.

"Good morning, Daddy," the kids replied.

"Get the bucket!" Eli said.

"Sure," I said. I opened the envelope and read the name.

The tenth name is Dad

I knew exactly who dad was. It was my dad. I had been thinking about my dad a lot. Ten years ago, he went to a nursing home. Looking back on what I know now, the signs were there that he struggled with mental health his whole life.

Ashley and I were newly married when he came to visit us. Something didn't seem right. He couldn't speak coherently and kept making noises. I didn't know what to do. He was staying at a local hotel while he was visiting. I tried to take him to the hospital, but he wouldn't go. I went with him to his room and ended up calling 911. They came to assess my dad. He gave them his name and birthdate but refused to go to the hospital. They said there was nothing they could do. I called my aunt, and she didn't know what to do either. I watched him in his chair laying there making strange noises.

My aunt finally said, "There is nothing you can do. Go home for the night and come back in the morning."

The next morning, I called the local police department and asked them to do a welfare check. I prayed that he would go with them to the hospital. I am not sure how it happened, but he agreed to go. I followed them to the hospital. My dad would never live on his own after that.

Emma interrupted my thoughts. "Is this you, Dad?" Emma asked.

"No. This is my dad, your grandpa."

Ashley nodded her head. She knew who it was too.

My dad lived in a nursing home 100 miles away in Clancy, Montana. When my dad went to the hospital it was one of the hardest days of my life. The whole thing was a blur. My dad didn't get better at first. He kept telling me he wasn't my dad when I would visit, and then he thought he was me. He ended up in a behavioral unit for a few weeks. Then, things turned a little better for him. He was able to get stable enough that the Clancy nursing home accepted him. He was diagnosed with schizophrenia.

Fortunately, my dad gave me power of attorney for medical and financial decisions a few years earlier. I sold his house and got rid of all his belongings. I remember having a garage sale and watching everyone go through his things. I had to leave. I couldn't take it. Ashley supported me and comforted me during this process. Every time I look at him, I know that it isn't him.

"I better get ready for work, and then I will go visit my dad," I told my family. Before I went to work, I grabbed an old photo album with pictures of him in it.

I left the house and arrived at work. "Good morning, Zach," I said.

"Good morning, Timothy."

I saw Buddy Brown hooking up his trailer, getting ready to leave. He turned to me, gave me a wave, and yelled, "Merry Christmas, my friend."

I waved back and wished him a Merry Christmas too. I had a feeling that would be the last time I would see Buddy.

Zach looked at me and said, "What name did you get today?"

"I don't know what you are talking about, Zach." He winked at me. I told him after work I was going to go visit my dad.

***

The roads were decent for December, just a little windy. Clancy is a beautiful town with huge boulders that border the mountains and cliffs.

I knocked on my dad's door and walked in. "Hi Dad," I said. He opened his big blue eyes and just stared at me. "How are you Dad?"

He kept staring at me. I took his hand and rubbed it. He rubbed my hand back.

"I love you, Dad."

I sat next to his bed and opened the photo album. I showed him pictures of himself riding motorcycles and snowmobiles. His face lit up. For a few minutes he understood that those were pictures of him. Then he sat back in bed, and put his hand in the air, to gesture no more. I put the album away.

I stayed in his room until the CNA came in and got him up for dinner. We walked to the cafeteria and ate together. Chicken and mashed potatoes. One of the employees cut his chicken up for him and brought him milk and orange juice. We didn't say a word. I just sat next to him.

When he was done, we walked back to his room. He laid down. I grabbed his hand and said a prayer. I knew that his parents were watching over him. He has his own angels. After a few more minutes, I said, "Bye, Dad, I love you."

As I walked out the room, I heard him say, "I love you too." Those were the first words he said to me that night.

That night I looked in the mirror and could see his face in mine. Ashley came up behind me and gave me a big hug. She didn't say anything. She didn't have to. I made sure I told her and the kids how much I loved them that night.

Before I went to bed, I called Zach to make sure he was doing okay.

16

Two Days until Christmas

I woke up multiple times that night. I couldn't stop thinking about my dad. I had just fallen asleep when the kids came in.

"Dad, time to get up."

Ashley grabbed my hand as we walked to the tree.

"I think we should all open the envelope today," I said.

Everyone placed their hand on the envelope, and we slowly opened it and read the name together. This time the envelope had multiple names:

The Eleventh names are Timothy, Ashley, Emma, Kaylee, and Eli

"Dad, my name is on there," Kaylee said.

"They all are. I know what we are supposed to do today," Ashley said.

"You do?" I asked.

"Yes, we are to serve each other all day. This is our day to spend together and take care of one another."

"I have to go to work today, but I will come right home when I am done. This whole day will be our day," I said.

"Yay!" Eli yelled.

"This is going to be the best day ever," Emma said.

"Good morning, Zach," I said. "Let's get this truck unloaded as fast as possible. I get to spend the day with my family."

"You bet, Timothy. I will jump in the trailer too."

When I got home, I walked through the front door and could smell bacon.

"Bacon!" I yelled.

"Daddy!" The kids came running up and gave me a big hug.

"Sit down at the table. We made you breakfast," Emma said.

"I flipped the pancakes," Kaylee said.

Eli smiled and gave me a hug.

"Hi honey, how was work?"

"Great, but I am so excited to be home."

"Yes, we made you a special late breakfast to start the day off right. I made a list of several things we can do today," Ashley said.

"Bacon, eggs, and pancakes. Best breakfast ever," I said. "What's on the list?"

"I am not going to tell you; it's a surprise," Ashley said.

After the best breakfast was over, we loaded into the truck.

"First stop is the duck pond," Ashley said.

"I got the bread," Eli said.

We spent an hour feeding the ducks. The pond was frozen, but a few stayed behind. The kids made sure the aggressive duck didn't hog all the bread. Then we went to the riverfront and walked along the path.

"Let's get a Hot 'N' Ready pizza for dinner. It will be like college," I said.

"College was only last month," Ashley said as we laughed.

"Since today is such a special day, let's get breadsticks too," I said.

Everyone yelled. I didn't know Eli could have a higher pitch than the girls.

"Wow. I hope my ear drums don't break," I stated.

"I do have a surprise for you tonight," Ashley said. "I found a place that shows old movies, and tonight they are showing 'It's a Wonderful Life.' Do you know why that is a surprise?" Ashley asked.

"Yes, how could I forget? That's the movie we watched when we first held hands. We had been dating for a few months, but we hadn't held hands yet. We went to a theater like the one we are going to now. When my finger touched yours, you grabbed my hand tight and said, 'What took you so long?'"

"That's right, why did it take you so long?" she asked.

"I don't know, but I won't take that long tonight."

And I didn't. When the movie started, I grabbed her hand tight and held it in mine while we watched the movie.

Emma asked, "Is it true that every time a bell rings, an angel gets its wings?"

"I don't see why not," Ashley said.

"I am going to get a bell and ring it once a day," Kaylee said.

"We need all the angels we can get," I said.

After the movie ended, we had ice cream.

"It's never too cold for ice cream," Ashley said.

"I love ice cream!" Eli shouted.

"These past days we have been serving other people. Today we were reminded that we need to always take care of each other," I said. "We will be together forever. We have many Christmases to come and memories to make."

"Let's go buy some lights and more ornaments for the tree," Ashley said.

We bought two strands of lights and a few bulbs to go on the tree.

Kaylee found a bell and asked, "Can we get this and put it on the tree so we can remember to ring it?"

"That is a great idea," Ashley said.

That night, we stood in our house looking at the tree decorated with a few homemade ornaments, the lights, some bulbs, a gold bell, and a shiny bucket under it.

"Let's read the story of Jesus' birth," I said.

"Yes, and let's dress the kids up," Ashley said, as she came out with bed sheets, towels, and some rope.

Eli was a little too big to be a baby and Ashley and I were a little older than Mary and Joseph. Emma was a young wiseman and Kaylee didn't have any sheep to shepherd, but that was the best reenactment of the birth of Christ I have ever seen.

Glory to God in the highest, and on earth peace, good will toward men.

Before I went to bed, I called Zach to make sure he was doing okay.

17

One Day until Christmas

Eli came into our room before four. "Time to get up," he said.

It was 3:45 a.m.

"Cuddle with us for a few minutes," Ashley said, yawning.

He laid right on top of me and wanted a kiss. After a few minutes of him moving all over us, we decided to get everyone up. We gathered at the tree and sang "Away in a Manger" before we looked in the envelope.

Away in a manger
No crib for a bed
The little Lord Jesus
Lay down His sweet head
The stars in the bright sky
Look down where He lay
The little Lord Jesus
Asleep on the hay

"I love that song," Ashley said. She bent down and grabbed the envelope out of the bucket. There was no money in it this time, just the envelope. She opened it and read the name.

The twelfth name is Jesus Christ

"I love Jesus," Kaylee said.

"What can we do for him?" Emma asked.

"I think we need to spend the day thinking about Jesus and looking for Him," I said.

"I agree. Let's spend the day trying to be more like Jesus. If we look, we can see His hand everywhere. Do you work today?" Ashley asked me.

"Yes, unfortunately, Christmas Eve is one of the busiest days for delivery companies. I do have tomorrow off. I will be home as soon as I can."

Zach was already in the building. Christmas music was playing, and cinnamon buns were in the breakroom.

"Merry Christmas!" Zach said to everyone.

One of the delivery drivers said, "Zach seems different. I am not sure what happened, but he looks so much happier."

Even though everyone was working on Christmas Eve they seemed happier than the other days. Zach's attitude was contagious and the environment at work was better. It was positive. People were being kind and helping each other. The morning went by fast.

As I drove off, I looked in my rearview mirror. I saw Zach's car and thanked Heavenly Father that Zach was in my life.

"We are making Christmas cookies," Emma said, as I walked inside.

"Yummy. Can I help frost them?"

"Yes," Kaylee said.

Ashley stood in the kitchen with an apron on and flour on the front. She was so beautiful. She looked like an angel. I was sure if I rang the bell on the tree that she would get her wings and fly away. I gave her a kiss and asked what I could do.

The phone rang and Ashley picked it up. "Yes. Sure. That sounds like a blast. What do we need to bring? See you then."

She looked at the family and smiled. "I know how we can serve Jesus today. I just got a call from Jodi from church. She got our number from Lynn. The family that was going to do the Nativity can't make it today and they need volunteers to help. The neighborhood the church is in is a local favorite for the community. The whole neighborhood puts luminaries out on every street. They spend all day putting sand in paper bags with a candle inside. At dusk they light them. Jodi said the neighborhood becomes magical. Cars line the streets. They turn off their lights and drive around. The church puts on a live Nativity, sets up luminaries around the grounds, and cars drive through the church parking lot and see the true meaning of Christmas.

Jodi asked if we could help get the luminaries ready. They want Dad and me to be Joseph and Mary and the kids to be in the background. They have all the clothes for us to use. They also will have a truck there taking donations for food share. She needs us at 1 p.m."

"Yay!" the kids said.

"I am going to be a sheep," Eli said. We laughed and Ashley picked him up and said, "My little sheep."

We had cookies for lunch; I didn't tell Ashley about the cinnamon buns for breakfast. We walked outside. It was snowing softly. On the way to the church, I saw neighbors filling bags with sand. Some of them were drinking hot chocolate and eating cookies. Everyone smiled. This place already seemed magical to me.

Jodi greeted us. "Hello, come over and get some hot chocolate and cookies."

I passed this time.

We spent the afternoon preparing the bags for Jesus. When it started to get dark the neighborhood lit up. Right at 5:30 p.m., the luminaries were lit. It was so exciting. Our family was all dressed and ready to be in the Nativity for Jesus.

At 6 p.m. cars started lining the streets. Some drove through the neighborhood first, and then through the church parking lot to see the Nativity. Some came right to the church. For three hours, different families came through taking pictures of the Nativity and watching for a few minutes, trying to think about what it was like the night the Christ Child was born.

I saw several people pass through. Ms. Smith drove with Avery and Robin in her car. Zach and Erica drove through. They smiled and waved at us. I even saw Bob and his wife, Kate. Crystal came through too. Greg came through with his family and said, "From one believer to another, Merry Christmas." I didn't see Buddy that night. He was driving truck somewhere, being everyone's buddy. I didn't see Jim or his friends, but to me they will never be nameless.

Then it hit me, we had given Jesus a gift every day, not just today. Every time we helped someone; we were giving a gift to Jesus. He used us as angels to deliver His gifts to them. As the last few cars drove through that night, I no longer felt like I was acting. I was there the night of Jesus' birth. It was real. It did happen, and even though it happened over two thousand years ago, it happens every day we let Jesus be born in us. I knelt and thanked God for the gift of His son.

The night was almost over. Jesus would be born in the morning. The food share truck was packing up. I didn't have food to donate, but I reached in my pocket and found a $100 bill.

I asked if they took money, "Absolutely," the man said, and he pulled out a shiny bucket for me to drop the money into.

"Did you see that?" Emma asked. "He has a bucket too."

"Yes, yes, I did."

We all stood in silence for a few minutes.

"I don't want this night to end," Kaylee said.

"Me neither," Eli said.

"It doesn't have to. Let's drive through the neighborhood," I said.

A few of the luminaries were burnt out and the cars were mostly gone, but most of the lights were still on. The magic of the night was still there.

***

"Good night, everyone," I said, as Ashley and I tucked the kids in.

"We didn't buy any gifts for them," Ashley said. "I hope the past twelve days have been enough of a gift."

"It will be enough," I said.

Before I went to bed, Zach called me to make sure I was doing okay.

18

There is Always a Name

Christmas morning came, we went to the bucket at 4 a.m., but it was empty.

"Let's put a name in it," Eli said.

"Great idea," I said.

Ashley grabbed some paper, handed pieces out with a pencil, and said, "Write down a name that you are thinking of and put it in the bucket."

"I am putting Lynn's name in," Eli said.

Just then, the phone rang. It was Lynn, she noticed our light was on and wanted to know if we wanted Christmas breakfast.

"Of course," I said.

We got dressed and went to Lynn's. When we walked in, we saw a beautiful tree. Under her tree, was a shiny bucket. Lynn saw me looking at the bucket and winked. I thought to myself, how many buckets are out there? And how many names are in those buckets? Not just during the Christmas season, but every day.

The magic bucket is symbolic of the Spirit of God and the revelations that come through the

whisperings of the still small voice. There is always
a name.

Twelve Names of Christmas

12. Teacher – Peace from not feeling able to help a child

11. Neighbor – Lights on their house

10. Co-worker – Listening to them as you find out they are suicidal

9. Nameless – The homeless that go unnoticed

8. Friend at church – Visit mom's grave

7. Sick Child – Christmas angels

6. Worst enemy – Basketball game

5. Person at the store – Introducing them to a friend

4. Truck Driver – An opportunity to stay one night in a town and make fond memories

3. My Dad – Visiting those with mental health challenges

2. Our names – Spending time with family and taking care of each other

1. Jesus Christ – Live Nativity and luminaries

42022335R00064